Marguerite's Fountain

Written by
Rachel Elliot

Illustrated by
Petra Brown

WITHDRAWN

HUTTON
hg
GROVE

For Serena
with love,
in celebration
of all the dancing.
R.E.

For Jan
my dear friend
P.B.

Marguerite's Fountain
Text Copyright | Rachel Elliot
Illustration Copyright | Petra Brown
The rights of Rachel Elliot and
Petra Brown to be named as the author and
illustrator of this work have been asserted by
them in accordance with the Copyright,
Designs and Patents Act, 1988

Published in 2016 by Hutton Grove
An imprint of Bravo Ltd.
Sales and Enquiries:
Kuperard Publishers & Distributors
59 Hutton Grove, London, N12 8DS
United Kingdom
Tel: +44 (0)208 446 2440
Fax: +44 (0)208 446 2441
sales@kuperard.co.uk
www.kuperard.co.uk

Published by arrangement with Albury Books
Albury Court, Albury, Oxfordshire, OX9 2LP

ISBN 978-1-857337-97-6 (hardback)
ISBN 978-1-857337-96-9 (paperback)

A CIP catalogue record for this book is
available from the British Library
10 9 8 7 6 5 4 3
Printed in China

Benjamin lived at the bottom of the tallest steeple in the cathedral yard. There was a little gap in the sturdy stone. It had been there for hundreds and hundreds of years.

1

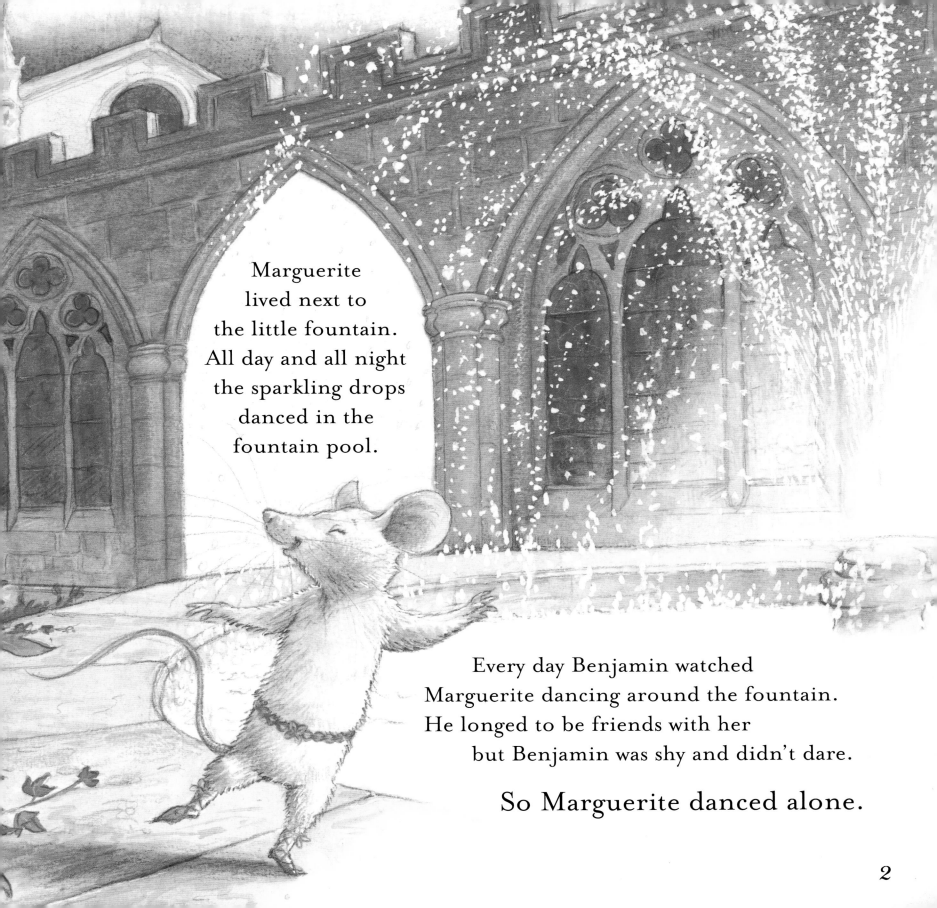

Marguerite
lived next to
the little fountain.
All day and all night
the sparkling drops
danced in the
fountain pool.

Every day Benjamin watched
Marguerite dancing around the fountain.
He longed to be friends with her
but Benjamin was shy and didn't dare.

So Marguerite danced alone.

Then, one day, someone
was dancing with Marguerite.
His name was Randolph.
His fur was dark and glossy
and his eyes were as
black as oil.

Randolph wanted to
have the little fountain
for himself.
"You are the most beautiful
dancer I have ever known,"
he told Marguerite.

3

Benjamin wanted to tell
Marguerite the truth.
But Randolph was big and strong.
Benjamin was small and scared.

"You have a beautiful voice."
So Marguerite danced for
Randolph and sparkled for him.
But he was lying.

So he said nothing.

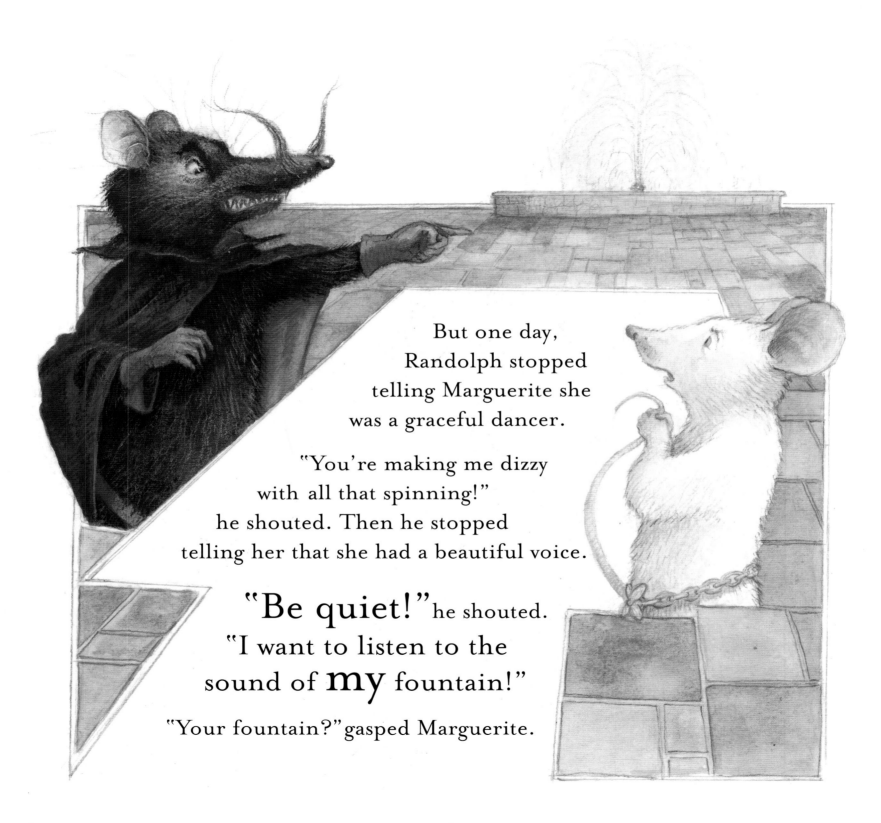

But one day,
Randolph stopped
telling Marguerite she
was a graceful dancer.

"You're making me dizzy
with all that spinning!"
he shouted. Then he stopped
telling her that she had a beautiful voice.

"Be quiet!" he shouted.
"I want to listen to the
sound of my fountain!"

"Your fountain?" gasped Marguerite.

Randolph twirled his thin mustache and laughed.

"It is my fountain now," he said. "You have to find somewhere else to live. The sewer is empty, you can live there."

Benjamin watched Marguerite creep away from her little fountain.

6

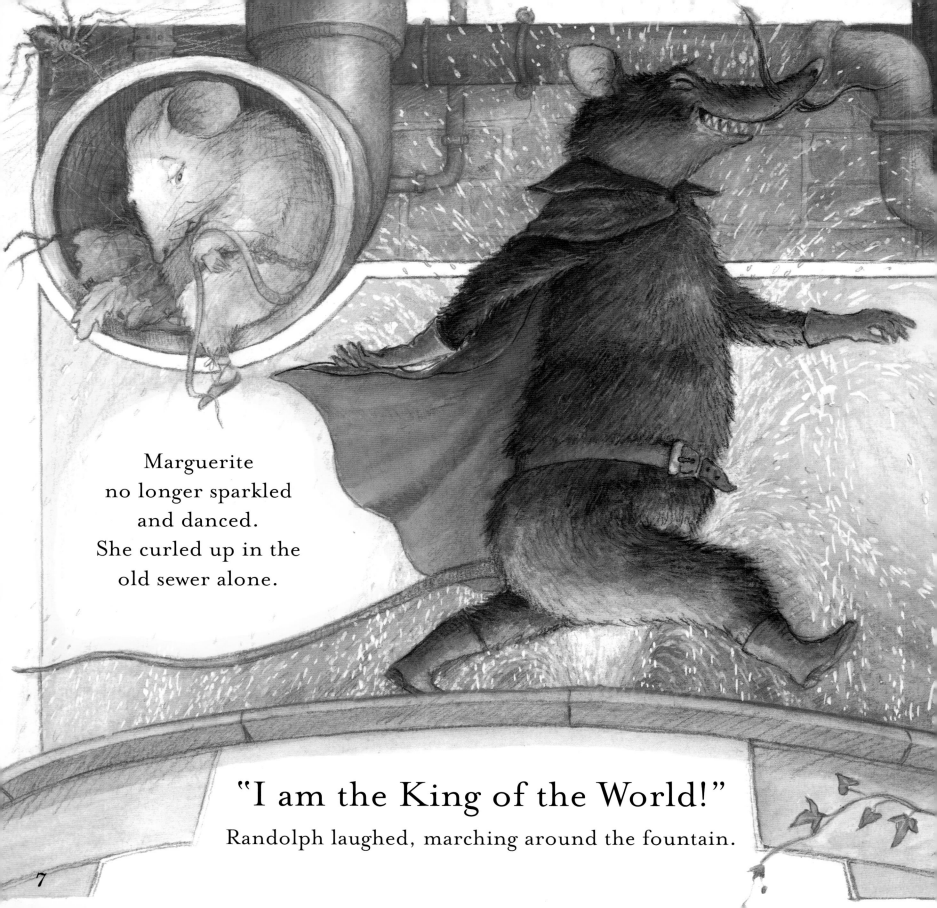

Marguerite
no longer sparkled
and danced.
She curled up in the
old sewer alone.

"I am the King of the World!"
Randolph laughed, marching around the fountain.

"I wish I was strong
and brave,"
sighed Benjamin.

Then he had
an idea.

8

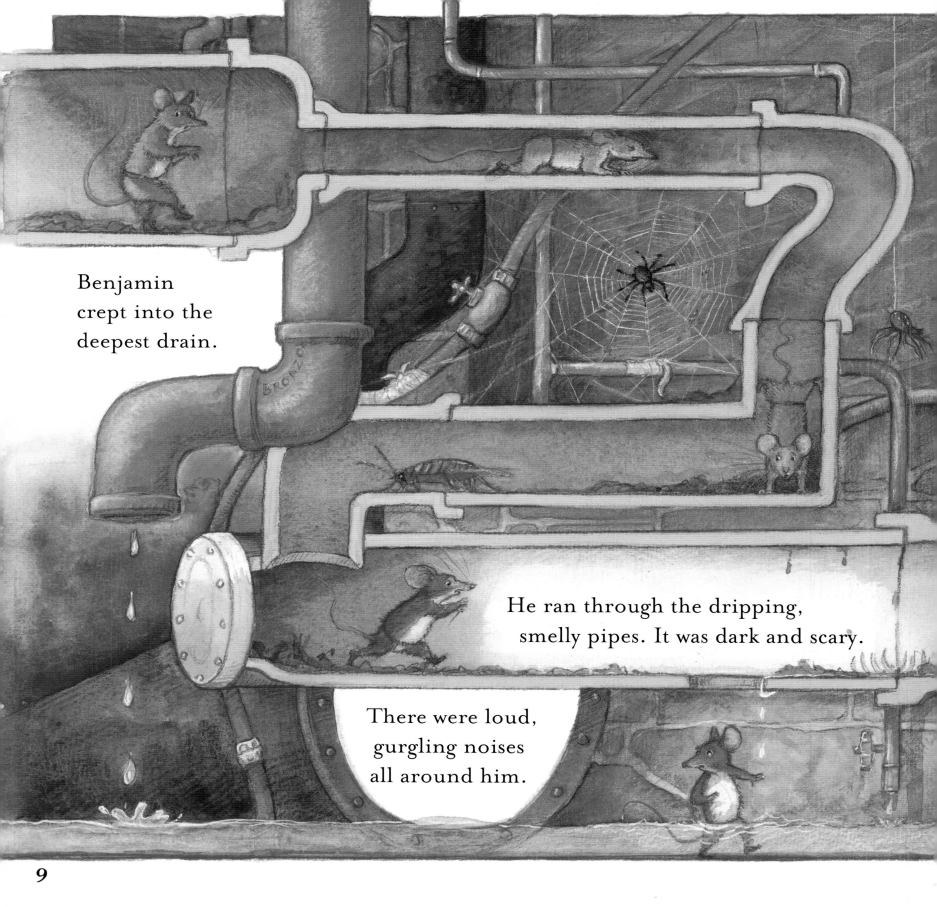

Benjamin crept into the deepest drain.

He ran through the dripping, smelly pipes. It was dark and scary.

There were loud, gurgling noises all around him.

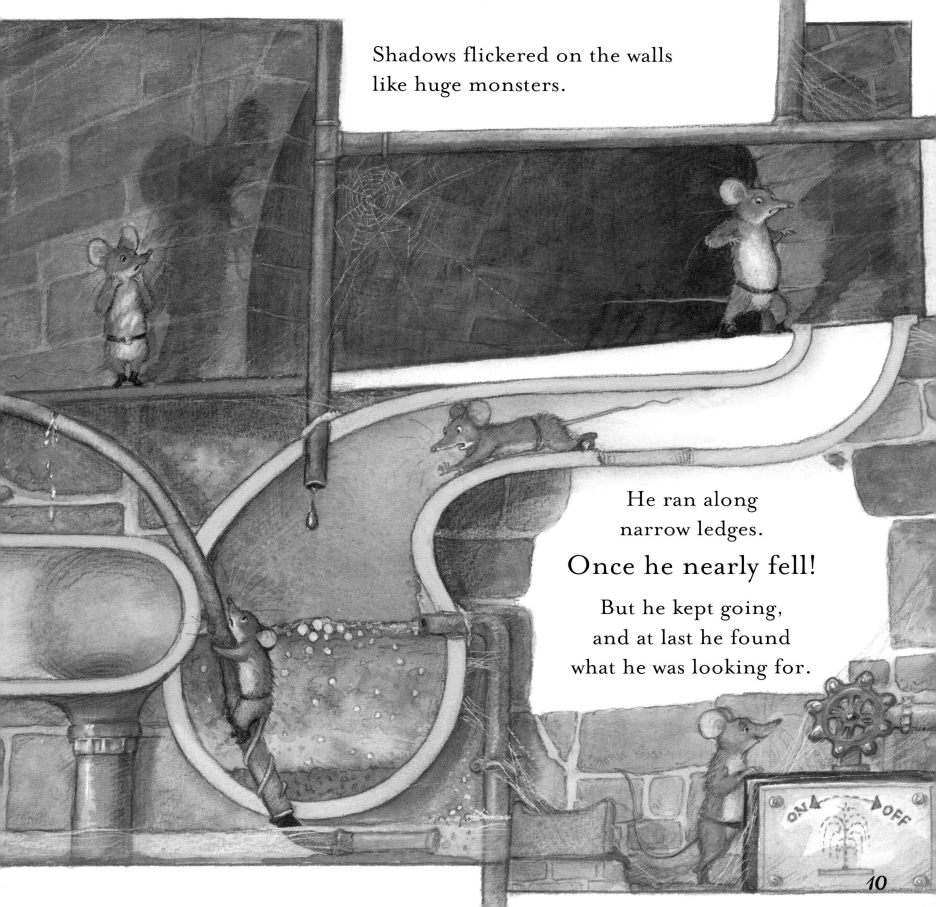

Shadows flickered on the walls like huge monsters.

He ran along narrow ledges.

Once he nearly fell!

But he kept going, and at last he found what he was looking for.

10

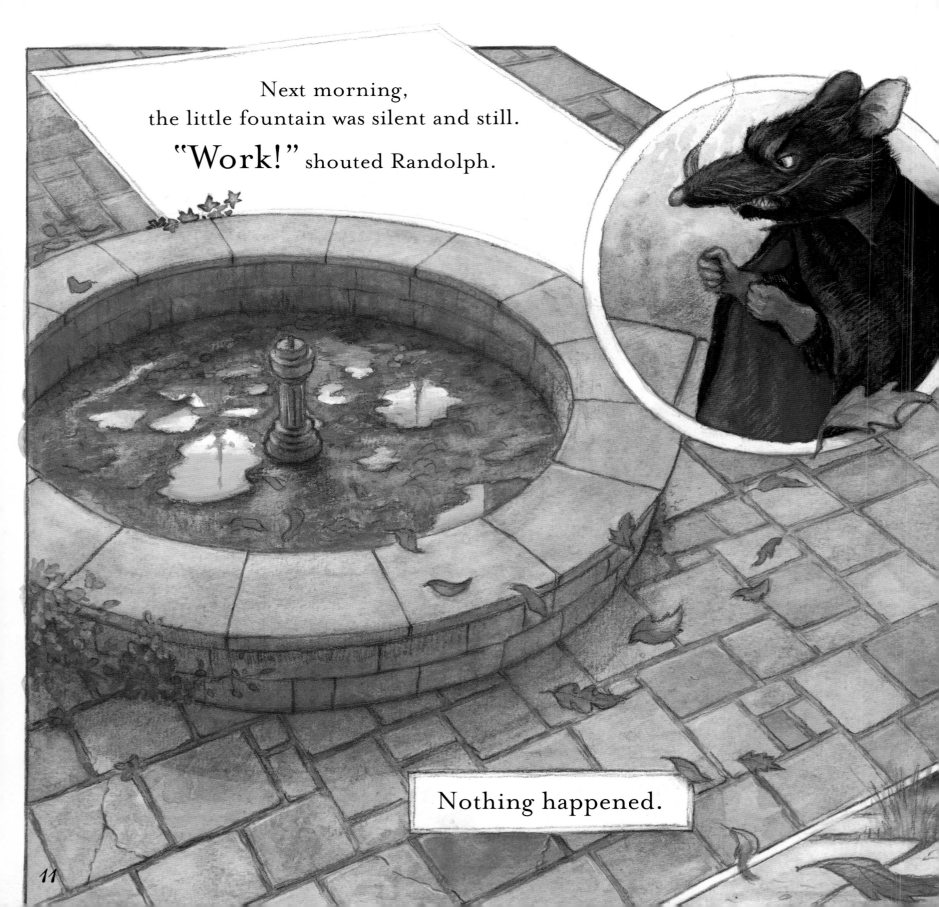

Next morning,
the little fountain was silent and still.
"Work!" shouted Randolph.

Nothing happened.

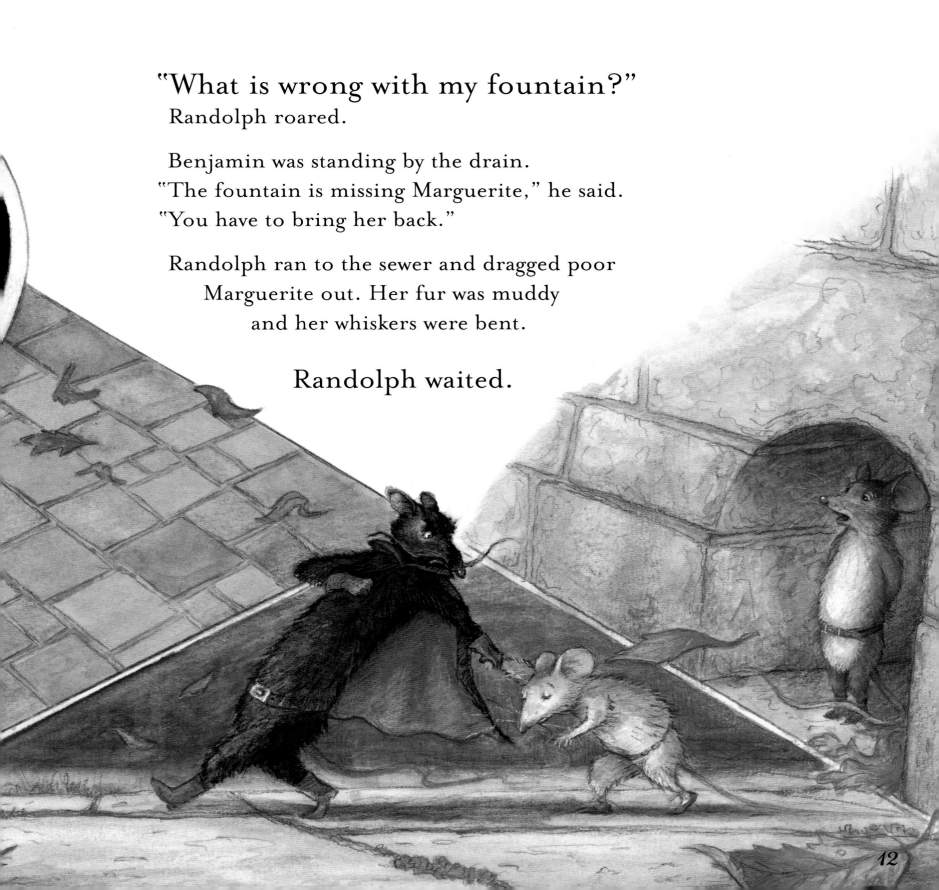

"What is wrong with my fountain?"
Randolph roared.

Benjamin was standing by the drain.
"The fountain is missing Marguerite," he said.
"You have to bring her back."

Randolph ran to the sewer and dragged poor
Marguerite out. Her fur was muddy
and her whiskers were bent.

Randolph waited.

But the fountain was
still and silent just like before.
"You lied to me!"
Randolph shouted at Benjamin.
Benjamin's paws were shaking,
but he hid them behind
his back.

"The fountain is
unhappy because
Marguerite is unhappy,"
he told Randolph.
"You have to be kind to her."

13

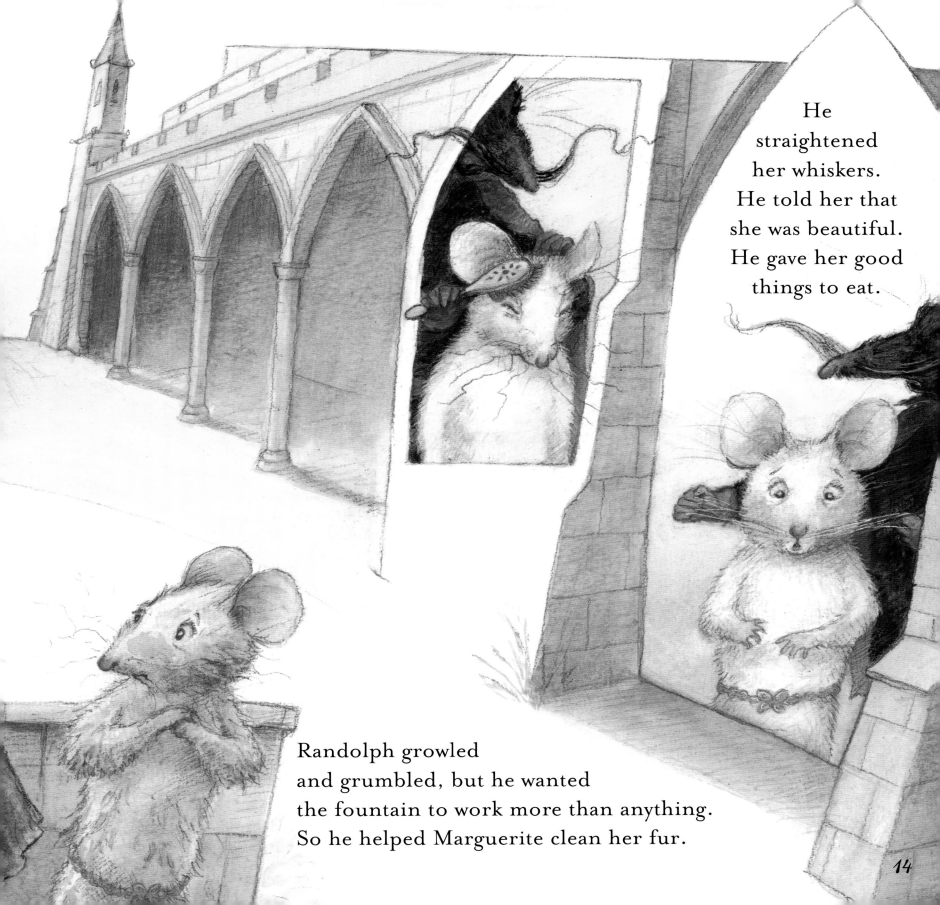

He
straightened
her whiskers.
He told her that
she was beautiful.
He gave her good
things to eat.

Randolph growled
and grumbled, but he wanted
the fountain to work more than anything.
So he helped Marguerite clean her fur.

14

But Marguerite did not smile or sing or dance.
And the little fountain was silent and still.
"You lied to me!" Randolph shouted again.
Benjamin was so frightened his little tail

was shaking.

Marguerite looked at Benjamin.
She could not bear to see
Randolph scare him.

"There is a little wheel at the bottom of the deepest drain," she said. "It turns the fountain on. But the drain is dangerous."

Randolph's oil-black eyes sparkled. **"I'm not scared of anything!"** he snarled as he squeezed his greasy body into the drain, and disappeared into **the dark.**

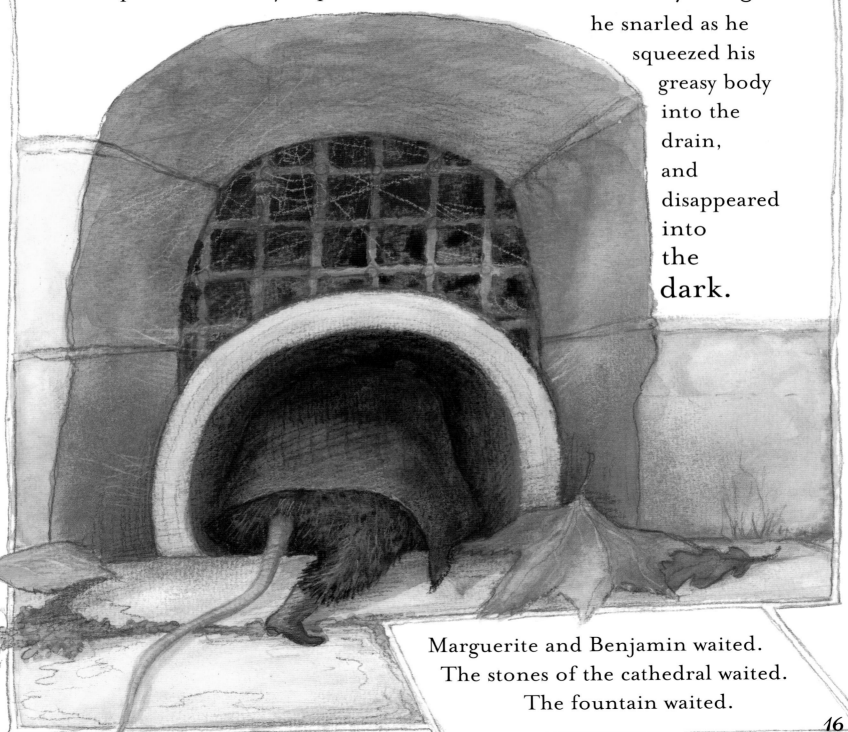

Marguerite and Benjamin waited.
The stones of the cathedral waited.
The fountain waited.

16

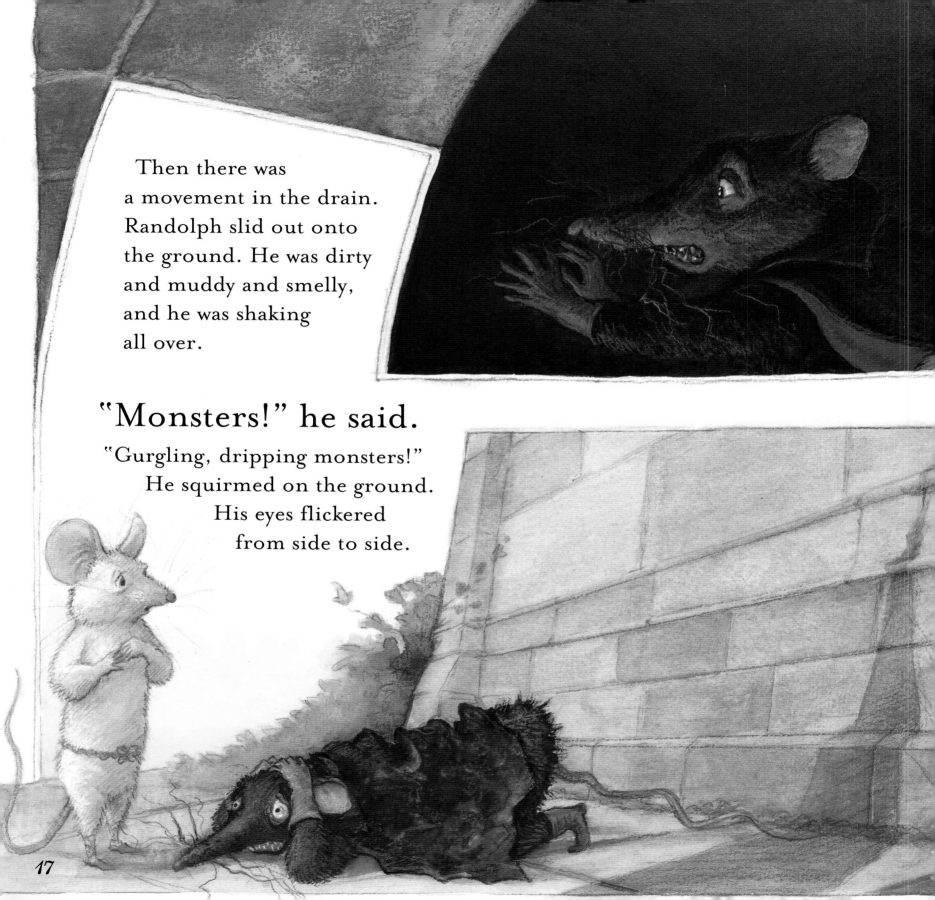

Then there was
a movement in the drain.
Randolph slid out onto
the ground. He was dirty
and muddy and smelly,
and he was shaking
all over.

"Monsters!" he said.
"Gurgling, dripping monsters!"
He squirmed on the ground.
His eyes flickered
from side to side.

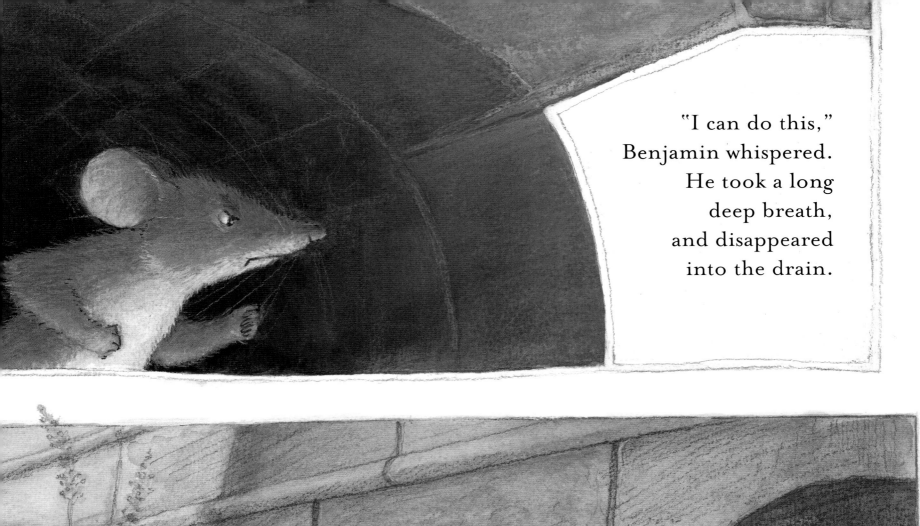

"I can do this," Benjamin whispered. He took a long deep breath, and disappeared into the drain.

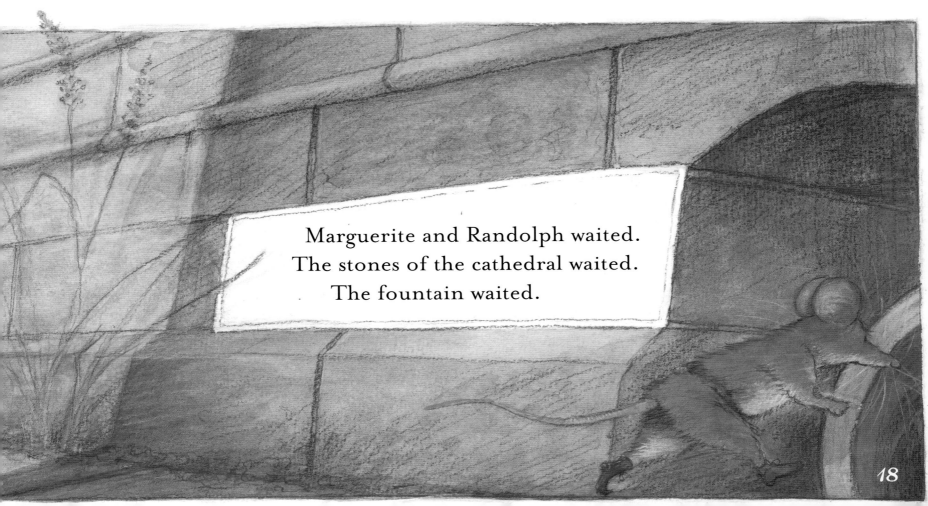

Marguerite and Randolph waited.
The stones of the cathedral waited.
The fountain waited.

At last, Benjamin stepped out of
the drain. He was dirty and muddy
and smelly, but his bright eyes
were full of fire.

"You are a coward!" he said.

"Your heart is as stony as the cathedral
and as tiny as a single drop of water!"

"This is my fountain,"
Randolph said,
his voice shaking.
"No!" said Benjamin.
"This is Marguerite's
fountain."

Suddenly the water started
to gurgle and bubble.

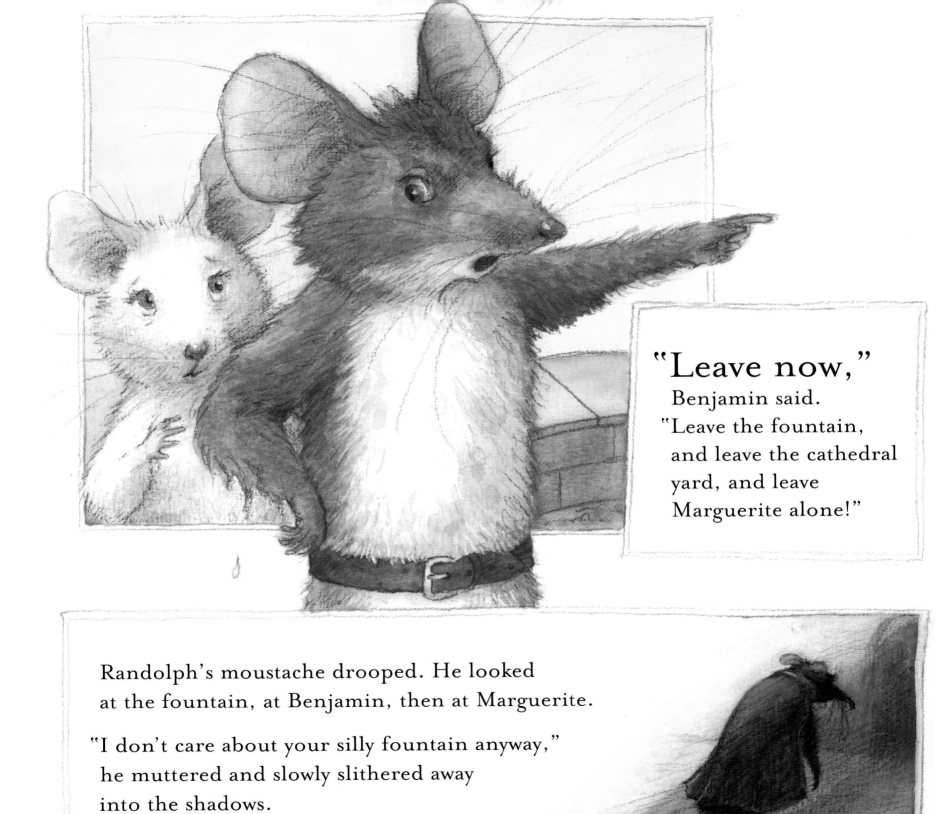

"Leave now,"
Benjamin said.
"Leave the fountain,
and leave the cathedral
yard, and leave
Marguerite alone!"

Randolph's moustache drooped. He looked
at the fountain, at Benjamin, then at Marguerite.

"I don't care about your silly fountain anyway,"
he muttered and slowly slithered away
into the shadows.

20

Then something
magical happened.

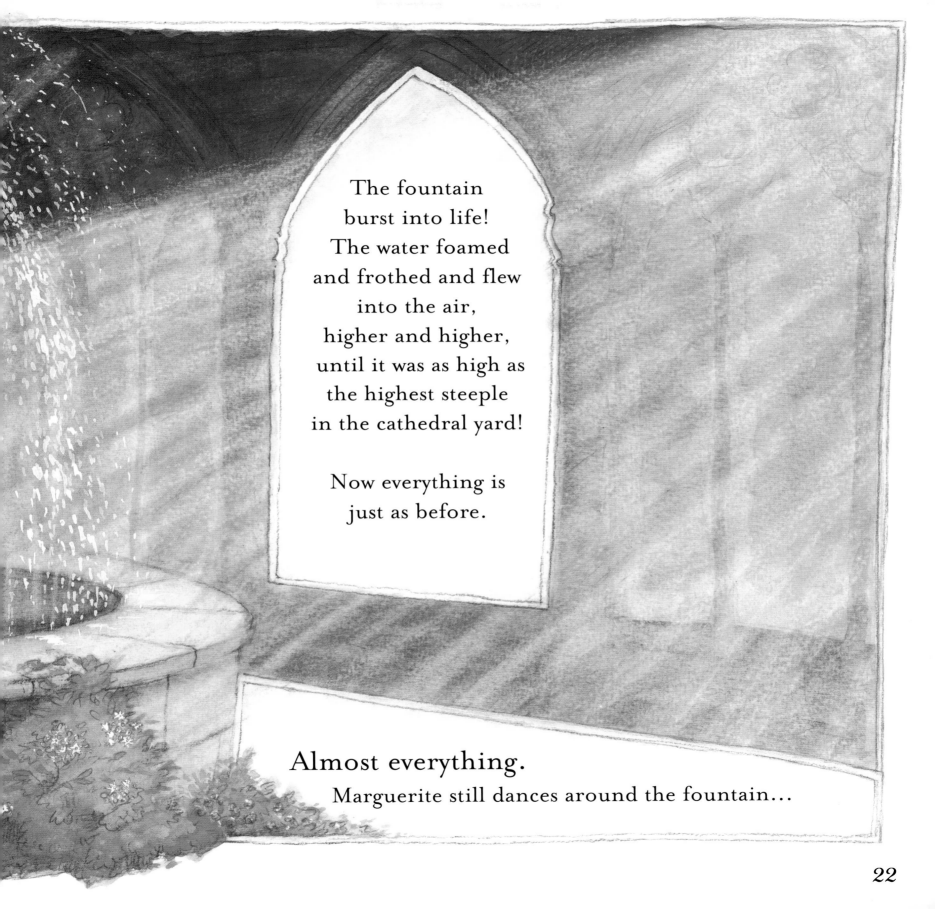

The fountain
burst into life!
The water foamed
and frothed and flew
into the air,
higher and higher,
until it was as high as
the highest steeple
in the cathedral yard!

Now everything is
just as before.

Almost everything.
Marguerite still dances around the fountain…

...But now
Benjamin dances with her.